My Naughty Little Puppy

New Tricks for Rascal

Boing!

For Robin ~ H.W.
For Eddie and Andrew ~ K.P.

WOOF
magazine

STRIPES PUBLISHING
An imprint of Little Tiger Press
1 The Coda Centre,
189 Munster Road,
London SW6 6AW

A paperback original
First published in Great Britain
in 2010

Text copyright © Holly Webb, 2010
Illustrations copyright
© Kate Pankhurst, 2010, 2012

ISBN: 978-1-84715-129-2

The right of Holly Webb and Kate
Pankhurst to be identified as the
author and illustrator of this work
respectively has been asserted by
them in accordance with the
Copyright, Designs and Patents
Act, 1988.

A CIP catalogue record for this
book is available from the British
Library.

Printed and bound in China.

10 9 8 7 6 5 4 3

For more information
about Holly Webb visit:
www.holly-webb.com

My Naughty Little Puppy

HOLLY WEBB

Illustrated by
Kate Pankhurst

Stripes

Chapter One

Rascal in Trouble

"Ellie! ELLIE!"

Ellie jumped, losing her place in the book she was reading. Max was yelling and he sounded furious.

She heard Max's bedroom door bang and then the sound of him thundering across the landing. "I haven't even been in his room," she muttered to Rascal, who was lying on the bed next to her while she read her book for school. Rascal's ears were pricked

My Naughty Little Puppy

up, and he was staring at her bedroom door. Ellie looked worriedly down at the puppy. "I haven't been in his room, but... Oh, Rascal, I hope you haven't gone in there and—"

Her bedroom door burst open, and her brother marched in, his face bright red with anger. He was waving something black and white, and squished-looking at her. "Look!"

My Naughty Little Puppy

"What is it?" Ellie's voice wobbled. Max was ten, two years older than she was, and he was usually very easy-going. But when he was angry, he could be really scary.

"You see! You can't even tell what it is! Because that stupid dog's eaten it! It's my football, Ellie! My signed Walchester United one that I queued for three hours to get!" Max chucked the football on the floor. "Or it was. It's just rubbish now."

"I'm really sorry..." Ellie felt her eyes filling with tears. "Did you leave your bedroom door open?"

"Don't try and make it my fault!" Max yelled. "It's your dog that chewed it up! I'm going to tell Mum, and you know what, Ellie? I'm going to say we should send

Rascal back to the dog breeder. He's the worst-behaved puppy in the world!"

Max stormed out, and Ellie stared after him, horrified.

Rascal whimpered, frightened by the shouting, and Ellie hugged him tight. "He didn't mean it," she whispered. "And Mum and Dad would never send you back."

But as she heard Max downstairs, telling Mum about why Rascal should go back to the breeder's, and Mum answer that she would think about it, Ellie didn't feel quite so sure.

The next morning, Ellie sat at the bottom of the stairs, pulling on her school shoes.

My Naughty Little Puppy

She wriggled her toes sadly. These shoes weren't nearly as comfy as the trainers she'd been wearing all through the Easter holidays. The time off seemed to have gone so quickly, with all the excitement of getting their new puppy.

Rascal sniffed at her feet curiously, and nibbled the end of the velcro strap with his sharp little white teeth.

Ellie gently pushed him off. "No, Rascal! Mum'll go mad if you eat my school shoes. You ate half of her sock yesterday, remember? And she still hasn't forgiven you for chewing her trainers."

Rascal looked up at Ellie, his eyes sparkling with mischief. There was just something about shoes!

My Naughty Little Puppy

"Are you ready, Ellie?" Mum asked, coming downstairs with Ellie's PE bag. Max and Ellie usually walked together. Their big sister Lila went in the other direction to go to her secondary school.

"Can you come too, so we can bring Rascal?" Ellie asked Mum hopefully, as she got to her feet. "I bet he'd love a walk. He's going to miss us."

"*I'm* not going to miss him," Max growled, as he stomped down the stairs. He was still really cross with Rascal.

Rascal had heard the word "walk" and was dancing around underneath the hook where his lead hung, barking excitedly.

"Oh, please..." Ellie begged. "Look at him, Mum!"

My Naughty Little Puppy

"Not now. Look at the time! You're going to be late if you don't hurry. But I'll bring him to meet you after school, OK?"

Ellie's best friend Christy was waiting for her at the school gate. "Oh, I was hoping you'd have Rascal!" she said, when she saw Ellie and Max running down the road.

"Mum said no, because we were late," Ellie panted. "But she's bringing him this afternoon so I can show him off to everyone!"

She told Christy all about Rascal and Max's football as they were putting their bags away in the classroom. "He still isn't talking to me, he didn't say one word all the way to school. And last night when Max said we ought to send Rascal back, Mum said she would think about it! Then Dad went out in the garden later and found this huge hole in the lawn..."

"Settle down, please, girls!" Mrs Harley, Ellie's teacher, looked over at her and Christy. "Less chatting, Ellie. Your literacy words are up on the board."

"Sorry," Ellie muttered, turning red. She didn't usually get told off at school. But she cheered up later on when Mrs Harley asked anyone who'd done something exciting over the holidays to share it with the class. Ellie stuck up her hand. Sometimes she was shy about speaking up in front of people, but she wanted everyone to know about Rascal.

"Yes, Ellie?" said Mrs Harley.

"We got a puppy last week. His name's Rascal."

"That's exciting." Mrs Harley smiled at her. "What sort of dog is he?"

"A Jack Russell. He's thirteen weeks old. My mum's bringing him when she comes to pick me up, you could come and see him."

Mrs Harley nodded. "I'd love to."

At break time lots of people from Ellie's class asked her about Rascal. She just couldn't wait to show him off. But she was a bit worried, too.

Christy nudged her as they sat back at their desk after break. "Are you OK?"

Ellie leaned closer to whisper. She didn't want to get told off by Mrs Harley again. "I'm just worried about Rascal. I hope he's not being naughty at home. Last time I left him he howled the whole time."

"Your mum's there, isn't she?"

Ellie nodded. "But he misses *me*!" She

couldn't help feeling a little glow of pride at that.

Mum looked a bit frazzled when she came to meet Ellie and Max. She was standing by the gate holding Rascal's lead very tightly. She tried to get him to shush, as Rascal started barking at a pushchair.

"Hi, Mum! Has Rascal been OK?" Ellie asked, crouching down to make a fuss of him. Rascal bounced up and down, trying to lick her face.

Mum sighed. "He howled all day. I've hardly got any work done. And look at his lead! He pulled it down off the hook and chewed it to pieces!"

"Oh no!" Ellie took the lovely red lead from her mum. It was now chewed all down one end!

Just then, Christy rushed over. "Hello, Rascal!" she said, crouching down and tickling him. The puppy frisked around her, his whole body wagging with his tail. Other girls from Ellie's class crowded round to take turns stroking him, too.

Ellie saw Mrs Harley coming over. "He's lovely, Ellie." She bent down to stroke the lively puppy, and he jumped up at her, yapping happily.

It was only when he turned round to be stroked by one of the other girls that Ellie noticed the trail of little muddy paw prints down Mrs Harley's beautiful pale pink skirt...

Ellie flushed pink. "Oh, I'm sorry, Mrs Harley, I didn't see he was muddy!"

Mrs Harley smiled. "Don't worry, it'll wash off. My dog's always doing that."

Ellie nodded, but she still felt embarrassed, and Mum hurried them through the school gates, before Rascal caused any more trouble.

On the walk home, Rascal sniffed every fence and lamp post, and soon he and Ellie were way behind Mum and Max.

"Come on!" Mum called. "I suppose at least he's walking now," she sighed, when Ellie caught up. "I had to carry him most of the way to school before!"

Chapter Two

The Courgette Catastrophe

That evening, Ellie was struggling with her science homework at the kitchen table, when she had a sudden thought. She'd let Rascal out for a wee earlier and he'd been in the garden for an awfully long time. She jumped up and ran to the window. She could just see a small, white shape, scrabbling away – in the middle of Dad's veg patch.

At that moment, she heard the front door open. Dad was home!

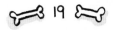

My Naughty Little Puppy

"What are you up to, Ellie?" Dad asked, as he walked into the kitchen and spotted her struggling to pull down the blind on the window. "Let me help with that," he said, coming over.

"It's OK, I'm fine," Ellie blurted out. But it was too late...

"Have you seen what he's doing?" Dad yelled, as he spotted Rascal through the window. He flung open the back door, and hared off down the path.

Ellie watched anxiously as Dad grabbed Rascal and stomped back indoors with the puppy tucked under his arm.

My Naughty Little Puppy

"He's dug up every single one of my courgette seedlings! I only planted them out yesterday!" Dad snapped.

"Sorry," Ellie whispered. "He just likes digging. He doesn't understand..."

Dad put Rascal down, and the puppy cowered under Ellie's chair.

"I know, Ellie. But he can't be allowed to dig everything up."

"He hasn't had as many walks today as usual, because I was at school," Ellie explained. "He was working off all his energy."

"We'll talk about this later," Dad said, and stormed off to have a shower.

Ellie looked down at Rascal, who was sitting under her chair. "What are we going to do, Rascal? That's Mum, Dad *and* Max, all cross with you."

Just then, Max came into the kitchen. He crouched down next to Rascal, and held out his hand solemnly. "Shake a paw, Rascal. All is forgiven."

"What are you doing?" Ellie asked, as Rascal licked Max's hand instead.

"He dug up all Dad's courgettes, Ellie! I *hate* courgettes! Do you think you could get him to work on the beetroot next?"

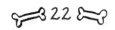

My Naughty Little Puppy

At least Max wasn't cross with Ellie and Rascal any more. But Dad had had a serious talk with Ellie that night, and Ellie was starting to feel quite worried. What if Mum and Dad *did* decide that Rascal was too naughty? Would they really send him back, like Max had said? She knew that Rascal had already had another home before they got him, with an elderly couple who'd found him too much of a handful.

"You're only a little bit naughty," Ellie told Rascal, as she brushed him out in the garden after school the next day. She'd noticed a lot of white hairs around, and she didn't want Mum and Dad to have anything else to be grumpy with Rascal about.

But as she let Rascal back into the

kitchen and put the grooming brush away, Ellie heard a howl of horror from upstairs.

Mum looked up from the vegetables she was chopping. "Was that Lila?"

Ellie stared down at Rascal. "Please tell me that's not because of you!" she whispered.

About ten seconds later, Lila burst into the kitchen. Her eyes were glittering with fury, and she pointed at Rascal, who backed behind Ellie.

"He ate my new pink lipstick!"

Ellie's eyes widened. "Oh, no—"

"And *then*," Lila went on, "he was sick all over my carpet!"

Ellie felt a terrible urge to giggle. It was awful but funny at the same time.

"I'll clean it up," she volunteered, hoping that might make Lila feel better. "And I'll buy you a new lipstick!" She gave a sigh. She had wanted to use her pocket money to buy Rascal a squeaky bone toy to distract him from digging.

"Clean it up together," Mum said. "And please be quick, girls. Your grandad's coming over for dinner, remember."

Lila grabbed the carpet cleaner and headed upstairs, muttering about horrible, smelly dogs. Ellie set off after Lila, closing the kitchen door firmly as Rascal tried to follow. Rascal gave a hurt little whimper, but Ellie didn't give in. He definitely wouldn't be welcome in Lila's room!

Mum passed Grandad a slice of cake, and gave him a serious look. "Have you any ideas how we can get Rascal to behave, Dad? He's being a bit of a nightmare."

My Naughty Little Puppy

Grandad bit into his cake and looked over at Rascal, who was sitting next to Ellie's chair and hopefully eyeing her portion. "Jack Russells can be tricky. They're really determined, which is what makes them such little characters, but it means it's hard to train them. I think you might need some help. Have you thought about puppy-training classes?"

My Naughty Little Puppy

Ellie smiled at Grandad. Puppy-training classes sounded like a brilliant idea!

But Mum looked thoughtful. "Isn't he a bit young? I'd planned to take him to some in the summer holidays."

Grandad shook his head. "No, not at all. The younger the better. Lots of classes have puppy time, when they just let the pups play together. That's really important for getting him used to other dogs, too..."

"Rascal always barks at other dogs in the park," Ellie put in. "Even if they're twice as big as he is!"

"I'll have a look online later and see if there are any local classes." Dad looked pleased. "But I think we all have to make a real effort to help Rascal to behave, too.

My Naughty Little Puppy

Making sure we don't leave things lying around for him to chew, stuff like that."

"And remembering to keep your doors shut!" Mum added.

Max made a grumpy noise through a mouthful of cake.

"And he needs more exercise and lots of fun play," Dad went on. "Puppy-training isn't going to stop him getting bored and digging holes, is it?"

Lila shrugged. "He's Ellie's dog, shouldn't she be doing all of that?"

Ellie beamed. She wouldn't mind that at all!

Chapter Three

The Dog-Training Disaster

With Ellie's help, Dad found a website for dog-training classes at the nearby village hall. He phoned the instructor later that evening and signed Rascal up to start at once. Luckily, there was a space in her beginners' class, which began on Friday, so they could start that very week.

Ellie was so excited. "Please can I come with you, Dad?" she begged, as soon as he got off the phone.

My Naughty Little Puppy

Dad laughed. "You've got to come! You're the only one who can get him to behave. If it was just me, he'd probably decide to lie down and sulk!"

Ellie giggled, but it was true. And it was a little bit worrying. What if Rascal didn't behave for her either? She frowned. That couldn't be allowed to happen. Mum and Dad already thought Rascal was a problem dog. He had to be a star at puppy-training, and prove that he was good enough to stay.

Ellie lay in bed that night, with Rascal curled up on her feet. (Mum had given up trying to get him to sleep in the kitchen.) She was in that dreamy state of half-asleep, and pictures of Rascal trotting perfectly to heel flitted through her mind. Rascal sitting

when she told him to – instead of looking
at her with a *Why?* face, like he did now.
Rascal fetching Dad's slippers... Ellie
giggled. Maybe not. The slippers would
definitely have holes in them when Rascal
had finished with them...

"Rascal, we're going somewhere really
exciting today." Ellie was sitting on the living-
room floor with Rascal after school on
Friday, watching TV. "And you have to be
very, very good, OK?"

Lila leaned over from the sofa. "Ellie,
why are you talking to the dog?"

Max sniggered. "She thinks he
understands."

My Naughty Little Puppy

"He does!" Ellie protested. She looked down at Rascal, who was staring at her with bright, clever eyes. She was sure he understood her serious tone of voice, anyway.

Ellie had already packed a bag with Rascal's favourite chew toy, the chicken-flavoured treats he really liked, a bottle of water, his bowl, and some plastic bags in case he had an "accident". She kept checking it, worrying that she'd forgotten something.

They set off as soon as Dad got home. That way they could fit in a quick run around the park first, so that Rascal wasn't too lively during the class – and had a chance to go to the toilet beforehand. But Ellie's nervous feeling only got worse as

My Naughty Little Puppy

she and Dad got to the village hall, and saw all the other puppies and owners.

Ellie spotted a girl with a neat bob, wearing a Chase Hill uniform going into the hall. "Oh! That's a girl from my school," Ellie whispered. "Amelia. She's in Year Six."

She had never spoken to Amelia, who was in the same class as Max, but she knew Max had said she was stuck-up. Amelia was with her mum, and they had a

beautiful King Charles spaniel, with huge, fluffy ears. Ellie wouldn't have been surprised if Amelia had blow-dried them for him.

"That's nice," Dad said.

My Naughty Little Puppy

Ellie looked horrified. "No, it isn't! What if we do it all wrong and she tells everyone at school?"

"I'm sure it will be fine," Dad said.

Unfortunately, he was wrong. As Ellie led Rascal into the hall, he dashed forwards, dragging Ellie along behind him.

"Come back, Rascal!" Ellie muttered, going red, as everyone turned round to stare. But Rascal had never seen so many puppies in one place before, and he barked himself silly, jumping up and down, and running in circles.

"Pick him up, Ellie," Dad hissed.

Ellie hugged Rascal tightly and tried to calm him down, but he kept yapping and trying to wriggle out of her arms.

My Naughty Little Puppy

"Don't worry." The instructor, Jo, came over to them, smiling. She was much younger than Ellie had imagined she'd be, with a long brown plait. "He'll soon get used to it. This is Rascal, isn't it? We're just going to start with everyone introducing themselves."

She gathered them all together, and Ellie looked round curiously at the other dogs. Rascal was definitely the smallest,

My Naughty Little Puppy

but they all looked quite young. As well as
Amelia and Goldie, there was a chocolate
Labrador puppy called Sam, a Dalmatian
called Libby, a Westie, Angus, who was
almost as small as Rascal, and Josh, a
Border collie pup. Jo had brought her
own dog too, a beautiful golden Labrador
called Emma, who looked like she knew
everything there was to know about
dog-training.

My Naughty Little Puppy

"These classes are all about you ending up with a happy, well-behaved dog," Jo explained. "A dog who gets on well with all your family, and other dogs too. So, we're going to start with some playtime. I think we'll put Libby, Sam and Josh together in one group. Then Angus, Goldie and Rascal in the other, as they're about the same size."

Jo moved the two groups to opposite ends of the hall, and told all the owners to crouch down. "That way your puppy knows you're nice and close if he's scared. We'll take their leads off and let them play with these rope toys. If one of the pups starts being too rough, just gently take them away for a minute, OK?"

Ellie undid Rascal's lead. He looked up

at her curiously, and then went to sniff the
rope. But Angus wanted it too, and as he
tugged it away Rascal barked loudly.
Everyone in the hall turned round to look.

Goldie had been sitting watching, but
now she tried to join in, and Rascal noticed
her for the first time. He trotted over, and
started trying to sniff her bottom!

My Naughty Little Puppy

"Stop him!" Amelia snapped. Ellie snatched him up, her face scarlet. After that, Goldie and Amelia kept giving Rascal identical disgusted looks, and Ellie felt like a worm. She was glad when Jo told everyone to put the puppies' leads back on, so they could practise walking to heel.

"Get your treats out, everyone. Remember, we want the dogs to enjoy training, and to want to do what they're told. So, when your dog is paying attention to you, reward him. When he's walking, have the treat just in front of his nose, so he follows along. Off we go." Jo got them all walking in a circle round the room.

Rascal's tail was wagging as he followed his favourite treat, and he looked as though he was enjoying himself. Ellie took a deep, relieved breath. Maybe he had just been getting used to this training thing!

Then Rascal bolted, pulling the lead out of her hand. Ellie squeaked and chased after him.

Rascal whizzed up the stairs to the stage, where everyone had left their bags, and Ellie gasped. She knew what he was doing. Jo ran lots of classes that evening, and she'd mentioned that she brought sandwiches to keep her going.

Delicious-looking chicken sandwiches, one of which was now hanging out of Rascal's mouth.

Chapter Four

A Bigger Dog-Training Disaster

"That's her, over there." Ellie pointed across the playground.

Christy stared at the group of gossiping Year Six girls. "Oh, *her*! I know who you mean now. Poor you!" Christy giggled. "I can just imagine Rascal sniffing her dog's bottom..."

"It was awful," Ellie muttered. "The whole class. I've been thinking about it all weekend. Jo said it didn't matter about the sandwiches, but I was so embarrassed, and Dad nearly made us go home before the end."

"Your dad's got a couple of days to get over it before the next one, hasn't he?"

"The next class is tomorrow. Tuesdays and Fridays. I've just got to try and avoid Amelia till then," Ellie added, hiding behind Christy, as Amelia glanced their way.

"Rascal will get it in the end," Christy promised. "I know he will."

Ellie frowned. "He's still being a monster while I'm at school, too. I'm really worried Mum and Dad are going to say he's too much for us. That's why it's so important that he's good at the training. And at the end of the lesson, Jo told us there's going to be a show at the last class."

"They did that at Bouncer's classes. He came second," Christy said proudly.

"Well, right now, Rascal would be about millionth, and there's only six dogs in the class," Ellie said gloomily.

"You need to teach him something really clever," Christy suggested. "A special trick that no one else knows. That would show everyone."

Ellie nodded thoughtfully. Now all she had to do was come up with the perfect trick.

On Tuesday, Ellie and Dad arrived at the hall at the same time as a boy about Ellie's age, who was leading the biggest dog Ellie had ever seen. His mum was

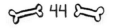

hurrying along behind them.

"Sorry!" the boy gasped to Ellie, as the enormous black-and-white creature squished him and Ellie together in the doorway. "Can't stop him!"

"Wow," Dad muttered. "That's a dog and a half."

The dog stopped just inside the door, and the boy apologized to Ellie again.

"He's so big! What sort of dog is he?" Ellie asked.

"He's a Great Dane," the boy said proudly. "He's called Hugo – because he's huge! And I'm Jack. We've just adopted him from the dog shelter."

"I'm Ellie, and this is Rascal. Is this the first time you've been to puppy-training?"

My Naughty Little Puppy

Jack nodded. "Yup. We were supposed to come on Friday, but we had to go to the vet's instead." He went red. "Hugo ate one of my socks."

Ellie giggled. "Rascal does that! And he chews shoes. We'd better not let them gang up."

Rascal and Hugo were already giving each other interested sniffs. Hugo was so giant that Rascal could fit underneath him with room to spare.

My Naughty Little Puppy

"Is it difficult, the training?" Jack asked nervously. "Hugo isn't very good at doing what he's told, and he's so big he just pulls me after him." Then he gave Ellie a fierce sort of look. "But I don't care. He's a brilliant dog, and I wasn't going to leave him in that shelter without anyone to love him."

Ellie nodded firmly. "I think he's great," she said encouragingly. "Look how nice he's being with Rascal." Then she sighed. "Honestly, you can't be worse than we are. My dad's hiding at the back, look, he's so embarrassed."

Jack chuckled, but then he looked anxious again as Jo called everyone to begin the class.

It helped a little that Ellie knew what to

expect, but Rascal didn't seem to have improved, even though she'd practised with him at the weekend. At least Amelia shared her disgusted looks between Ellie *and* Jack this time. Hugo was so big that if he went the wrong way, everyone knew about it.

"Let's do the 'sit' command now," Jo called near the end. "Hold the treat over the puppy's nose, and move it back so your pup naturally sits down. Say 'sit' clearly and firmly as he sits, and reward with the treat."

Ellie frowned. Jo made it sound so simple. Rascal wagged his tail delightedly as she got out the treats. She held one carefully over his nose, and started to move it back.

For a second it looked like it was about

My Naughty Little Puppy

to work, and then Rascal fell over backwards. He bounced up again with a confused little "Wuff!" and Ellie heard Amelia tittering. Goldie was sitting perfectly, of course.

Jack held his treat over Hugo's nose, but he had to reach up to do it because Hugo was so tall. Hugo wagged his tail enthusiastically and simply ate the treat out of Jack's hand. Amelia giggled again.

"Lots of practice is the key thing," Jo told them encouragingly. "Just five minutes, two or three times a day. They'll get there. Now, has anyone got any behaviour problems they want to talk about before the end of the session?"

Ellie looked down at Rascal. He'd done so many naughty things recently, she wasn't sure where to start. But then Ellie remembered how Rascal was still howling whenever she left him, and how Mum was hardly getting any work done. She looked around nervously, wishing somebody else would go first, but everyone was silent.

"Um, Jo?" She waved a hand. "Rascal barks and whines a lot while I'm at school. It drives my mum mad!"

My Naughty Little Puppy

Jo looked thoughtful. "Have you tried giving him one of your sweaters in his basket?" she asked. "Jack Russells can be very devoted to one owner, and if he thinks he's looking after something for you, he might be happier to be left."

Ellie smiled. "Thanks, Jo."

"Right. See you all on Friday," Jo called, and everyone started to gather their things.

Amelia walked past Jack and Ellie, smirking. "Bet you're glad you've found another dog that's as useless as yours," she sneered, as she made for the door.

Ellie gasped, and Jack stared after Amelia with his mouth open. "What's with her?" he said at last.

My Naughty Little Puppy

Ellie shook her head and smiled at him.
"She's just a mean girl from my school.
Rascal and Hugo are going to be brilliant
by the end of the course."

Behind her back, Ellie had her fingers
crossed.

Chapter Five

Ice Cream for Rascal

"So did Jo's tip about the jumper work?" Christy asked. It was Saturday, and Ellie and her mum were having a picnic in the park with Christy, her mum, and Christy's little sister Jade.

Ellie nodded. "Yes! I gave Rascal my old pink hoodie, and Mum says he hardly whines at all now! Jo's so clever. I said thank you to her at the class on Friday and asked if she had any more tips for Rascal.

She said it was just all about working with the dog and finding their strengths." Ellie sighed. "But I'm not sure what his strengths are, apart from guarding pink tops! I wish he was getting better at the rest of his training, too."

Christy nodded. "But Bouncer took ages to crack dog-training," she pointed out, scratching Bouncer's ears. "Didn't you, boy? And he's a Lab, they're supposed to be good at it! I'm sure Rascal will get there."

Ellie stared at Rascal, flat out on his back on the grass, with his paws in the air. "I hope so. I still need to find a special trick to teach him, just to show everyone how clever he is. He *is* clever, you know. He must be, to think up so many ways to be naughty..."

My Naughty Little Puppy

"Girls, would you like an ice cream?" Christy's mum called.

"Ooh, yes, please!" they answered.

Everyone got up to stroll over to the ice cream van, and Rascal perked up at the sight of food. As the girls took their ice creams, Rascal wagged his tail eagerly.

"I can't, Rascal," Ellie whispered. "Mum's watching!" Ellie's mum was very strict about not giving him anything that wasn't his proper food.

"You wouldn't like it anyway, Rascal," Christy told him. "It makes your teeth cold."

But Rascal continued to wag his tail hopefully. He couldn't reach Ellie's ice cream, or Christy's, but there was another one, very close to his nose.

My Naughty Little Puppy

Christy's three-year-old sister Jade was wandering slowly back to the picnic rug. Her ice cream was dripping temptingly.

As Ellie took another lick of her ice cream, Rascal suddenly pulled the lead from her grip. He then whipped round and snatched the ice cream out of Jade's hand.

My Naughty Little Puppy

"Heyyyy!" Jade wailed, as Rascal bounded off. "My ice cream! He took my iiiiice cream!" And she started to howl, even louder than Rascal could.

"I'm sorry, Jade! Please don't cry. We'll get you another one," Ellie promised.

Ellie's mum hurried over, looking horrified. "Ellie! How could you let him do that?"

Mum gave Ellie the money to get another ice cream, and took Rascal's lead while Ellie hurried off. Meanwhile, Rascal was busily licking up his stolen ice cream, slurping it out of the cone with big swipes of his pink tongue. He shivered deliciously as he finished it. Then he picked up the cone delicately in his teeth, and offered it back to Jade.

My Naughty Little Puppy

Jade shook her head.

"Urrgh, no, Rascal!" Ellie said, as she returned with the new ice cream and took his lead back from Mum.

Jade started to laugh. "He doesn't like cones! *I* don't like the cones too!" She giggled.

Ellie couldn't help laughing with her. At least Jade wasn't upset any more. But Mum still seemed furious.

Chapter Six

The Roast Chicken Incident

"We need something brilliant to show Mum you're a genius dog," Ellie told Rascal, as she took him into the garden on Sunday morning. She wanted to try out the trick she'd found in one of her dog magazines. "Believe me, Rascal, we've got a lot of making up to do. You are not Mum's favourite pet right now. And we only *have* one pet! I still can't believe she made me pay her back for Jade's ice cream out of my

pocket money yesterday. I don't know how I'm ever going to be able to save up to get you a new lead before the dog show."

Rascal watched with his head on one side, as Ellie took a dog treat out of a packet. "Look, Rascal. Your favourite chicken kind!"

Rascal gave an eager little whine.

Ellie carefully put the treat on his nose. "Don't eat it! I said *don't* eat it... Oh well. Let's try again."

My Naughty Little Puppy

Rascal licked his chops, as Ellie placed another treat on his nose. This was a good game! He was almost cross-eyed trying to see it, and his tongue was creeping out of his mouth.

"No, no, wait till I say! Oh." The treat had already disappeared, and Rascal was watching her eagerly for more. Ellie sighed. "I suppose we just need to keep practising."

Mum was just about to start preparing Sunday lunch, and had called Max, Lila and Ellie into the kitchen. "You will all behave beautifully, OK?" she told them. "This is the first time Auntie Gemma's brought her new boyfriend round."

"Yes, Mum." Max rolled his eyes.

"What's he called again?" Lila asked.

"Liam. And please make sure the dog behaves too," Mum added.

Ellie nodded frantically.

"Now, it would really help if you could all stay out of the kitchen while I make the roast."

Ellie slipped out into the garden with Rascal and his grooming brush, and the dog treats. She was determined to get the trick right eventually.

"I'm sure you kept it on your nose longer that time," Ellie murmured, as Rascal gobbled down another treat. "Let's have a break. Shall I make you look beautiful?" She started to brush Rascal lovingly, making sure his white coat gleamed. "We need to

My Naughty Little Puppy

show you off to Auntie Gemma and Liam."

Just then, Mum called. "Come in, please, Ellie. They'll be here in a minute. Oh Ellie," she sighed. "Look at you, you're covered in hairs! Go and change. I need to change too, actually." Mum looked down at her apron. "The chicken can just stay on the side and rest. Lunch is all ready, except for the roast potatoes."

"It smells great." Ellie sniffed the delicious roast chicken smell, as she headed out of the kitchen. Mum was obviously making a big effort for this Sunday lunch.

Ellie went upstairs to change her top. She was just coming back down when the doorbell rang. "I'll get it!" she called.

Auntie Gemma was standing at the door with a nice-looking dark-haired man, who seemed a bit nervous.

"Hi, Ellie! Liam, this is one of my nieces. Ellie's the one who really loves dogs."

Liam smiled at Ellie. "Gemma tells me you've just got a puppy."

Ellie nodded shyly. "Yes, he's called Rascal."

My Naughty Little Puppy

Dad popped his head out of the living room to say hello, and Mum hurried downstairs. "Hi, Gemma. It's great to meet you, Liam. I'm just going to sort out the lunch, it's nearly ready." She disappeared into the kitchen. Then there was a sudden scuffling noise, and everyone in the hallway clearly heard Mum shriek, "Oh no! Bad dog!"

"What is it?" Ellie cried, dashing after her.

But as soon as she got into the kitchen, she could see. Rascal was sitting at the bottom of the step stool Mum used for the high cupboards, looking really guilty. And in his mouth was what was left of the chicken.

My Naughty Little Puppy

"Honestly, I really do love fish fingers," Liam told Ellie's mum. "*And* they're delicious with gravy."

Mum smiled, but she still looked really upset.

Ellie felt so guilty that she hardly spoke during lunch. She knew how hard Mum had worked on the meal, and then Rascal had gone and ruined it. At least he hadn't got anywhere near the pudding, which was an enormous chocolate cake.

Mum had banished Rascal outside, and now Ellie could hear him whimpering and scratching at the back door, as she helped her with the washing-up.

My Naughty Little Puppy

"I suppose you'd better let him in," Mum sighed.

"I'm really sorry," Ellie whispered.

Mum gave her a hug. "I know. And it's my fault, anyway. I've told all of you so many times not to leave anything where Rascal can get it. I just didn't think about him climbing the step stool!"

"He's a master-criminal!" Ellie said, opening the back door for Rascal. But he didn't look like a master-criminal. He looked lonely and miserable, as if he'd hated being shut out. He slunk through the door with his tail between his legs.

"Oh dear, now I feel guilty," Mum said sadly.

Ellie shook her head. "He was really

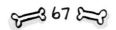

naughty, Mum. I think Liam likes dogs,
though. Can I go and show him Rascal?"

Mum nodded, and Ellie called Rascal
to follow her into the living room.

"Here, boy!" Liam reached down to
stroke Rascal, and Rascal beat his tail on
the floor, sitting happily at Liam's feet.

Ellie gave a sigh of
relief. Perhaps Rascal
was going to make
up for the chicken
incident.

"So, how old
is he?" Liam
asked, tickling
Rascal behind
the ears.

My Naughty Little Puppy

"About three months—" Ellie started to say, but then she broke off. "Rascal? What's wrong?"

Rascal was making strange coughing noises, and his little shoulders were heaving.

"Oh no! The chicken!" Ellie squeaked.

"Liam, move your feet!" Max yelled.

But it was too late. Ellie gasped in horror as Rascal gave one more huge cough and threw up the stolen chicken, all over Auntie Gemma's new boyfriend's feet.

Chapter Seven

The New and Improved Rascal?

Ellie was feeling really hopeful about Tuesday's class. She had been making a big effort with Rascal to try to make things up to Mum after the disastrous Sunday lunch. Whenever she had a spare moment, she walked Rascal to heel, and practised "sit", "down" and "stay". *And* she'd been working on their special new trick. Rascal still ate the treat before he was told, but at least he seemed to know he wasn't supposed to, which was a start.

So her heart wasn't thumping quite as fast as usual when she and Dad and Rascal walked into the village hall. Jack waved to her, and Hugo swung his thick tail joyfully as he spotted his friend Rascal.

"Let's start with our 'walking to heel'," Jo called, as the owners and their puppies got in line. "I think everyone's getting this now, aren't you? Lovely, Jack and Hugo!"

Ellie watched enviously as Hugo paced round the hall at Jack's side. He looked so grand and solemn, as though he was thinking carefully about every footstep.

She set off, hoping that they would do just as well. But Rascal wasn't in a serious mood at all. He was bright, bouncy and full of energy. Instead of walking calmly on a loose lead, watching Ellie for his treat, like he was supposed to, he was twirling and scampering around her. Ellie had to keep calling him back to his place.

"Ellie, don't get frustrated with him. You're doing well," Jo called. But Ellie felt like crying. Like Jo had said, everyone else was getting it right, but Rascal was worse than ever. How could he be so silly now, when he'd been doing so well in their practices?

Suddenly, Rascal darted around her legs again, and Ellie's eyes were so blurred with tears that she tripped over his lead.

Ellie landed with a thump. "Ow," she cried, as she hit her elbow hard on the floor.

Dad hurried over. "Ellie, are you OK?"

Ellie nodded, but her elbow ached horribly.

Rascal crept over to her, looking guilty. He gave Ellie's hand a lick, as if to say sorry, and then he nosed at Ellie lovingly.

"That dog is so useless," Ellie heard someone say, and she glanced up to see Amelia talking to her mother.

 73

My Naughty Little Puppy

Ellie rubbed her sleeve over her eyes. They thought her lovely Rascal was *useless*.

"Oh, Ellie! You really went down hard there," said Jo, coming over to check on her. "Are you hurt?"

"Not really," Ellie muttered, struggling up with Dad's help, "I just banged my elbow."

"You sit down," Dad said. "Have a rest. I'll take over for a bit."

Rascal looked confused when Dad took his lead. He sat down, pulling back on the lead, and staring at Ellie.

"Go on, Rascal." Ellie nodded to him, and reluctantly he got up to follow Dad.

Ellie sat in the corner and watched Dad with Rascal. They were meant to be practising "sit", but Rascal wasn't really watching the treats that Dad was holding over his nose. He would sit nicely, but then spring up to look round at Ellie.

Jo came to talk to Ellie again at the end of the class, crouching down beside her.

My Naughty Little Puppy

"How's your elbow?"

"Fine," Ellie muttered. She felt so bad – and the worst thing was that she'd really thought Rascal would be better this week.

"Ellie, I know you're finding it difficult with Rascal right now, but he will improve, I promise you. What's brilliant is that you haven't given up, and you're still being patient with him. I can tell you've been practising, too. That's really good. You should be very proud of her," she added to Dad.

Ellie managed a very small smile. Jo was being so nice, but Ellie wasn't sure she believed her.

Maybe Amelia was right about Rascal.

Chapter Eight

Ellie Downhearted

"You can't give up!" cried Christy. It was morning break on Wednesday, the day after Ellie's awful class, and she had just finished telling Christy the whole dreadful story.

"Haven't you been listening?" Ellie thumped her hand on the arm of the bench they were sitting on. "Ow. That hurt. Amelia was right, Christy. Rascal was useless. He wouldn't do any of the commands properly, and he made me look totally stupid in front of everyone." She shuddered. "I don't even want to think about the show."

"So that's it?" Christy looked horrified. "You're going to stop training him?"

"I'm not *training* him!" Ellie said wearily. "I'm just being dragged all over the hall by him!"

Ellie heard the sound of someone laughing, and looked up to see Amelia walking towards the bench. "I'm so glad you're giving up, Ellie. Saves me a job. I was coming to tell you that you really have to stop puppy-training. You're just ruining the class for everyone else."

"I'm not," Ellie said, but then her voice wavered. She gulped and blinked back her tears. She would *not* let Amelia make her cry.

"You waste Jo's time when she ought to be helping the others," Amelia went on.

"That's what training's for," Christy snapped. "Dogs who actually need it. If you're so perfect, why are you in the beginners' class?"

"Goldie is a beginner too, but she does what she's told. That little rat of Ellie's is never going to learn anything."

Ellie bounced up. "Rascal is not a rat! He's a beautiful dog, and you're just *mean!*"

"Yeah, Rascal's gorgeous, and clever, too," Christy put in. She grabbed Ellie's hand, and squeezed it.

Luckily, the bell went just then, and Amelia turned on her heel and stalked away.

But as they walked back into class, Ellie was pink-cheeked with fury. "I'm not giving up now," she told Christy. "We're going to show her. I *will* get Rascal to learn, even if we have to practise every minute of the day!"

Mum brought Rascal to meet Ellie and Max from school, and Ellie made an extra-special fuss of him. Christy joined in, too. Then Jessie and Lydia from their class came over and wanted to stroke him, and Rascal started to get really excited, jumping and yapping, and scrabbling at their legs.

Ellie asked Mum to pass her the packet of Rascal's special treats. "Sit," she said firmly, holding a treat above his nose. And he did! Rascal stopped yapping, and sat beautifully for the girls to pet him.

"Good boy!" Ellie was so pleased she felt like giving him the whole packet.

Christy rolled her eyes. "I thought he

hadn't learned anything, and you were giving up?"

Mum overheard. "Ellie! You can't! You've done so well with him. He walked to school beautifully, even when one of those big lorries he usually barks his head off at drove past."

"See?" Christy nudged her.

Ellie nodded. "I suppose it's been happening gradually and I haven't noticed. But he really was terrible in yesterday's lesson."

"Everyone can have bad days," Mum said firmly. "It's just a pity you'll have to miss the next class."

Ellie looked up at her in horror. "What do you mean?"

"Oh, Ellie," Mum sighed. "Didn't you listen to what Dad said this morning? He's got to go to a meeting on Friday, and he won't be back in time. I'd go, but Max has a football match, and I'll have to take him."

Ellie felt desperate. She couldn't miss the class! Not when Rascal was finally getting the hang of it. What if he forgot everything?

She had a brainwave as they passed Grandad's on the way home. "Mum, can I ask Grandad to take us?" she asked hopefully.

"That's a good idea." Mum nodded. "Let's go and see if he's in."

Grandad was delighted with the idea, and said he'd been meaning to ask if he

could come and watch a lesson. He
promised to pick them up in plenty of time
on Friday.

Ellie told Grandad all about her problems
with Amelia, and about Jack and Hugo on
their way to the class. "I'd never seen such
a big dog. You just won't believe the size
of him," she said. "About fifty times bigger
than Rascal."

Grandad nodded. "I love Great Danes. They're so gentle."

But even though he had been warned, Grandad still gasped at the sight of Hugo.

"Has he got bigger since Tuesday?" Ellie asked Jack, laughing.

Jack nodded. "He's growing so fast. But he still wants to sit on my lap like he's tiny! Is this your grandad?"

"Nice to meet you, Jack. I'm looking forward to seeing what you can both do," Grandad told them, sitting down at the side of the hall. "Don't look so worried, Ellie. Rascal's going to be brilliant." He beckoned her close and whispered, "Which one's that Amelia you told me about?"

Ellie pointed to Amelia and Goldie, and

My Naughty Little Puppy

Grandad nodded. "Mmm. Looks snotty. And that spaniel's nervous, look at her ears twitching. Rascal may be naughty, but he knows he's loved, and that's important. Don't let her bother you." He folded his arms firmly.

Somehow, having Grandad there to watch, smiling as they walked to heel down the hall, and giving her an approving nod when Rascal sat first time, was really encouraging.

Ellie gave him a hug at the end of the class. "You were a huge help," she said. Then she added shyly, "Grandad, I've got this special trick I'm teaching Rascal for the dog show. I put a treat on his nose, and he doesn't eat it until I say he can. Well, that's what's supposed to happen, he hasn't got it quite right yet."

Grandad looked thoughtful. "Sounds like it could take rather a lot of practice."

Ellie sighed. "I know, and there's not much time before the dog show. I just want Rascal to be perfect."

Grandad put his arm round her. "I think perfect's a bit boring, myself."

Chapter Nine

Stage Fright

At the next class, Jo reminded everyone that the show was next Tuesday. This lesson, they were going to go through the tests they'd be doing.

"Me and Rascal will come last in everything," Ellie muttered to Jack.

Jack shrugged. "Only in the tests Hugo doesn't. Come on, it'll be fun."

Dad seemed to think so too. He told Mum about it as soon as they got home.

"You don't need to come and watch. I don't think it's going to go very well," Ellie told her worriedly. "I'll be nervous, and I'm sure that makes Rascal naughtier."

But Mum had other ideas. She announced at breakfast the next day that the whole family would go.

"Ellie's been working really hard," she said when Max tried to protest he had football practice. "We need to be there to support her and Rascal."

Ellie had a piece of toast halfway to her mouth, and it stayed there as she froze in horror. "But I don't want everyone to come and watch," she blurted out.

Lila nudged Ellie. "What's up? You've gone really pale."

My Naughty Little Puppy

"I think I might be sick," Ellie muttered. "It's going to go horribly wrong and everyone will laugh at me."

Lila looked at her thoughtfully. "I'm sure it'll be OK. Rascal's been quite good recently. When was the last time he ate something he shouldn't have?"

Ellie nodded. "I still feel sick, though."

Ellie was giving Rascal a last groom in the garden just before the competition, to make him look perfect. She had spent the whole weekend practising and hoped Rascal would be on his best behaviour.

"There. At least you *look* beautiful," she told him, smoothing his lovely ears.

Lila came down the path. "Found you. Look, I've got you a present."

"Me?" Ellie looked surprised.

"You and Rascal. Because you've been so nervous about the show. Go on, open it!"

Ellie tore open the pretty pink paper, and hugged Lila. "A new lead! Oh, Lila, it's fab! Now he won't have to wear his chewed one."

My Naughty Little Puppy

"And a new red hairband for you, look. You can wear it with that red stripy T-shirt, and then you and Rascal will match."

Ellie tried on the hairband, and Lila nodded approvingly.

"You're the best sister," Ellie told Lila, hugging her again. "I feel loads better already."

There were lots of dogs at the show. Jo had put her three beginners' groups together to make it more of a competition. Ellie and Rascal were last in each section, just after Jack and Hugo. Waiting was making her nerves even worse. The judge, a lady called Anne, looked so serious as she took notes.

But when it was finally Ellie's go to show off walking to heel, Rascal did it perfectly, even though he was jumpy. Ellie saw Grandad making thumbs-up signs at her, and beamed at him.

After that, Rascal had to let the judge stroke him, to show that he was friendly. At least that wasn't something Rascal had a problem with, Ellie thought proudly, as Rascal charmed the judge with little wags of his tail.

But now, as they waited for their next turn, Rascal started to prance about, whining excitedly.

"Take him for a little walk outside if he's getting bored," Jo told Ellie, as she saw her trying to calm Rascal down. "I've just said the same thing to Jack and Hugo. I'll send someone to call you when it's getting close to your turn to show off 'sit' and 'stay'."

Ellie nodded gratefully. The village hall had a field and some trees at the back, so she headed out that way. She could see Jack jogging towards the trees with Hugo, and she set off after them.

"Let's go, Rascal!" she said encouragingly. But Rascal had other ideas.

The hedge that ran around the side of the hall was full of interesting smells, and he dug his claws in firmly.

"Rascal, come on," Ellie tried to sound fun and bouncy, but Rascal shook his head hard and suddenly twisted out of his collar, racing away towards the hedge.

Ellie chased after him. She could see his little white tail sticking out of the hedge, and she reached in and grabbed him carefully with both hands.

As she pulled him out, she gasped. Her beautiful, perfectly groomed puppy was absolutely covered in thick, smelly mud.

"Rascal!" Ellie wailed. "What have you done?" She looked back at the village hall, her eyes wide with horror. Any minute now

My Naughty Little Puppy

she was supposed to show off Rascal
doing his "sit" and "stay". He couldn't
possibly go back in like *this*!

Chapter Ten

The Great Dog Clean-Up

"Wow, what happened to him?" Jack said, coming up behind Ellie. Hugo leaned over to sniff the muddy little thing in front of him.

"He ran off and went digging under the hedge. What am I going to do?" Ellie shook her head. "I'll have to take him home. He won't even get his certificate for the end of the course! Oh, Rascal..."

"You can't do that." Jack frowned. "Look, can't we sneak him into the loos and wash the mud off?"

Ellie looked at him hopefully. "Could we? I suppose that's the good thing about a really small dog." She took off her jacket, and quickly wrapped it round Rascal – with the waterproof on the outside against his muddy fur. "There's no way we could smuggle Hugo anywhere!"

Jack grinned. "Not unless we walked him along on the far side of an elephant. Come on, Hugo and I will go and stand guard in front of the door to the ladies until Jo comes to call us for our turn."

Ellie dashed into the toilets, carrying her wriggly, whining bundle. She removed the jacket and placed a cross-looking Rascal into a washbasin.

"Sorry," Ellie told him, as she turned on the taps. "Bathtime."

Ellie started rinsing off the mud. But it was getting everywhere, and Rascal wasn't helping. He kept trying to jump out of the basin, and he was so slippery!

Ellie looked up in horror as the door opened, but it was only Lila.

"Mum sent me to look for you and I ran into your friend Jack as he was on his way into the hall. He said you were in here. Oh no! How did Rascal get like that?"

"He found a muddy hedge, you know what he's like. Please, Lila, help me wash him!"

Lila groaned, but she nodded. "I'll hold him. You can't let him get you muddy too."

My Naughty Little Puppy

She grabbed hold of Rascal, which left
Ellie free to swoosh the water over him.
Quite a lot of it went over Lila as well.

"What do you think?" Ellie asked at last.

"He has to be clean." Lila grinned.
"There can't be any more mud on him, most
of it's on me, and just look at the colour of
the water."

Ellie sighed. It did look as though she'd been trying to make mud soup in the basin, and Lila was covered, too.

"Here, you hold him under the hand dryer, I'll rinse the basin out." Lila handed her a wet, wriggly Rascal. "Dry your T-shirt, too!"

Rascal seemed to like the warm air from the dryer. He closed his eyes blissfully and stopped struggling.

Ellie fixed his collar and lead back on. Then she tried to give her muddy sister a hug, without getting too close. "Thanks, Lila!"

"Let's go," Lila said. "It'll be your turn any minute."

Jo was just looking for them as they went back into the main hall. "Ellie, you're on next, OK?"

My Naughty Little Puppy

It seemed as though the emergency bath session had washed away Ellie's butterflies, too! There was no time for nerves now. She and Rascal stood in the middle of the hall, ready to show what they could do.

"Sit!" Ellie smiled as Rascal sat beautifully. "Good boy, Rascal! Down! Down, Rascal!"

Slowly, Rascal lowered his tummy to the ground.

"Stay." Ellie moved a couple of steps backwards.

Rascal looked up at Ellie, and wriggled after her on his tummy. Ellie tried not to laugh. "Stay."

Rascal laid his nose on his paws.

My Naughty Little Puppy

"Good boy!" Rascal sat up again, and Ellie gave him a treat. She gazed down at him sitting there so nicely. He looked so clever... It was time for his special trick.

She took another treat and balanced it on his nose. Rascal's little tail thumped the ground, but he didn't eat the biscuit. He watched Ellie, his eyes hopeful.

"Eat it! Good boy, Rascal!" He finally

My Naughty Little Puppy

gobbled down the treat, and Ellie threw her arms around him. She couldn't believe he'd done it!

"That was great, Ellie!" Jo said, and even the judge smiled. "OK, Rascal was our last dog today, so now we're going to give out certificates to everyone, and Anne has chosen the winners. So, can you all come and stand in a line."

My Naughty Little Puppy

Ellie cuddled Rascal, and beamed over at her family, who were all clapping.

"Third place, Jack and Hugo!" Anne announced.

Jack gasped.

"Jack's done so well learning to control such a big dog," Jo commented, as she handed Jack a yellow rosette.

"Second goes to Amelia and Goldie."

Amelia didn't look happy, as she was given a red rosette. Obviously she'd thought she would come first.

First place went to a lady with a retriever, from one of the other classes. Ellie knew he had been the best dog in the show, and she certainly hadn't expected to win first prize, but she still felt a bit sad. It would have been so nice if Rascal had won *something*.

"And we also have a special award – we don't give this one out every time. It's Most Improved – and this is for Ellie and Rascal. Ellie's worked so hard with Rascal, and Jack Russells aren't easy dogs to train. So well done, you two!"

My Naughty Little Puppy

Ellie and Rascal came to the front, and Jo handed Ellie a green rosette.

"Oh, Rascal, you little star!" Ellie hugged him, and clipped the rosette on to his collar. He was so little that the ribbons trailed on the ground, and he turned round to try and nibble them. Ellie couldn't wait to show Christy. Hopefully, there would still be some rosette left by the end of school tomorrow.

My Naughty Little Puppy

"Well done, Ellie!" Mum hugged her. "Shall we sign up for the next set of classes? You've got three weeks before they start."

"Yes, please! Jack and Hugo are doing them, too."

"Do they teach emergency baths?" Lila whispered. "You'd be good at that."

Back at home, Mum went to make something for a celebration supper. Dad took off his trainers and frowned at the shoes lined up by the door. "You haven't seen my other slipper, have you?"

"Rascal?" Ellie looked down worriedly as she took off his lead. He stared back at her, wrinkling his nose. His eyes were

My Naughty Little Puppy

sparkling naughtily, as he trotted off across the hallway. He burrowed under the shoe rack, one of his favourite hiding places, and came out with the slipper. He held it up to Dad, like the most perfectly trained slipper-fetching dog ever.

My Naughty Little Puppy

"Good boy, Rascal!" Dad said in a surprised voice. "You've done so well today."

Ellie grinned. She decided not to point out the pattern of little teethmarks round the heel.

Like Grandad said, perfect could be a little bit boring!

WOOF

magazine

My Naughty Little Puppy

Playtime for Rascal

From best-selling author
HOLLY WEBB

It's School Sports Day and Ellie is worried she'll be last at everything. But then she comes up with an excellent idea – she can practise for all the events with Rascal! Will Rascal save the day?

Trick treat!

Once your dog has learned to obey the command "stay", you can teach him how to balance a treat on his nose – without munching it! This trains your pooch to listen more attentively.

For this trick, you'll need a packet of treats or biscuits and lots of patience!

1 – Tell your dog to sit and show him the treat. This gets his cooperation!

2 – Hold your hand under his chin and keep it there. Use your other hand to gently level his muzzle.

3 – Look into his eyes and firmly say "stay". Maintain eye contact and keep repeating this word.

4 – Carefully place the treat on his nose. Make him wait for a moment, then say "go". He'll instantly snap it up!

5 – Increase the time you make your dog wait during step 4 until he holds it long enough for you to take a picture!